Praise for SQUAR

Sheryl McGinnis has done it again. Sheryl has the unique ability to create books that will elicit conversation and dialog between an adult and child. Sheryl weaves her personal family story into one that a creative adult can use to begin helping a child understand the dangers of drugs and alcohol at an early age. If you have a young child, it is time to get started on The Addiction Monster and the Square Cat.

Larry Golbom, R.Ph., MBA, host of the Prescription Addiction Radio Show, Tampa, FL

The author hit the mark here with a cleverly disguised educational piece. This book has many valuable lessons. I now have a better understanding of what addiction does not only to oneself, but to an entire family and I hope I never put mine through anything like that. I will always remember that NEVER to start is the key.

Kate Clunn, Age 15, Ocean City, NJ

I learned that drugs and alcohol can cause an addiction. It only takes one time to become addicted. It begins to take control of your life and you struggle each day to try and stop it. Take it from The Square Cat — drugs make you unhappy and they make everybody that loves you unhappy too. This book was a good lesson for me to have enough self esteem to JUST SAY NO.

Talia Stokes, 12 years old, Weymouth MA

"I thought the book was good. It really told me that drugs are bad and that they could really hurt you. What I also liked was that they had Pumpkin the cat telling the story.

Hunter Penrod, Age 10, Santaquin, UT

"The Addiction Monster and the Square Cat," is a perfect title as this itself creates a great inquisitiveness to what the problem is. Beautifully done by the Author, Sheryl Letzgus McGinnis. Comfortable and educational. Reading for ages 10 to 12 and up.

Layne Robertson, 8 years in Education,
Company Director Tokyo, Japan

A great tragedy of our modern life is we can no longer allow our children to indulge themselves as children. In "The Addiction Monster and the Square Cat" McGinnis has bridged a gap by subtly weaving the perils of addiction with a child's story. Congratulations to the author for providing such a unique approach to combating an all too present and pervasive social ill.

Graeme Archer, Father and Grandfather,
Sydney Australia

The Addiction Monster and The Square Cat

A book for children about the dangers of drugs as told by Pumpkin, The Square Cat

By Sheryl Letzgus McGinnis

Dedicated to my two loving sons, Dale Ian McGinnis, Scott Graeme McGinnis, RN, and to my incredible husband Jack, for his encouragement and belief in my books.

This book is also dedicated to children everywhere who have wisely chosen not to do drugs.
I applaud you!

Other books by Sheryl Letzgus McGinnis

I Am Your Disease (The Many Faces of Addiction) - Outskirts Press

Slaying The Addiction Monster - Booksurge Publishing

Read Sheryl's articles about addiction online at www. Ezine.com

Scott and Marmalade, one of my brothers. They loved each other but I'm not jealous because I know I was Scott's favorite! I am so adorable.

SECTION ONE

Boo!

Did I scare you?

No, probably not. You like to be scared, don't you? I know you enjoy scary movies and reading about monsters and playing scary video games, right?

Well, let me tell you about another kind of monster, one who doesn't have big scary fangs or red eyes or horns sticking out of his head, or…

Oh wait…before we get to the monster, the villain in our little story, please allow me to tell you about myself. I'm sure you're wondering why I'm called the Square Cat. I'm not really square as you've probably already guessed.

You see, I'm a beautiful big, fluffy orange cat (not square at all but pleasantly plump and sort of round) and instead of having 9 lives (that's not really true anyway, we cats have only one life just like humans) I am lucky enough to have 9 owners. Actually it isn't quite that many but still I am taken care of and loved by many people.

The story takes place once upon a time, not so long ago in a lovely little community called Fairview.

Fairview isn't a very big place and everybody knows everybody. In the middle of Fairview is the town shopping center and in the middle of the shopping center is a really cool park with nice benches (just perfect for sunning myself while my people play in the park).

There are streets that go from the edges of the little town to the park. There are four of these main streets, one in each corner of the park, forming a square.

You're already ahead of me but wait, let me set my story up for you. The park is called The Square by all the locals and has been called that since the beginning of World War II, a very long time ago.

The school buses arrive at The Square in the morning and take all the high school kids to school because our town isn't big enough to have a high school; just grade school from kindergarten through 8th grade.

I was born in a house that was right on The Square and lived there until I was about six weeks old when my mother and my brother and sister and I were dumped off in The Square because nobody wanted us anymore. I don't know what we did wrong. We tried to be good, but the humans took us to The Square anyway.

There we sat in a box snuggled up with our mom who fed us as best as she could. We were warm because winter hadn't arrived yet. We were lucky because we were only there overnight. The next morning as all the kids were getting on the school bus somebody spied our little box and heard us mewing. One of the boys walked away from the school bus and came over to our little box, lifted the lid and got a big grin on his face. I knew I liked him right away.

He waved at his friends who were waiting on the bus and then he picked our box up and carried us to his house.

When we arrived at his house, he was greeted by a lady who wanted to know why he wasn't in school and what was in the box he was carrying. The lady started to get very angry with the boy until he opened the box.

As soon as the boy lifted the lid, I looked up at

him and did my best to look really cute and adorable (which wasn't too hard because I really am one cute cat!).

I would learn later that the lady's name was Sherry and she was the boy's mom. She had really kind eyes and a soothing voice. When she looked at me I gave her the biggest and loudest purr that I could. She smiled and stroked my head. I had a good feeling about these two humans.

"Mom, look at them aren't they beautiful?" the boy said. "You know we have to keep them, right?"

"No way Scott" said his mom. Ah, I know the name of my rescuer now.

"We'll keep one but we can't keep them all. I'll call my friend, Joan, and see if we can talk her into taking the mama cat and the two kittens. I know Joan will give them a really good home, that is if she'll agree to take them," Sherry promised.

Then Sherry called Joan to come to the house to see us beautiful kittens and our mama that somebody had left at The Square.

Before Joan arrived to come look us over, Scott picked me up and put me aside in another room, away from my mama and brother and sister. I was very confused but happy to be in a nice home with two very kind people.

Later, "Look at this beautiful mama cat and her two kittens" I heard Sherry say through the closed door.

"Oh they're beautiful and so sweet" Sherry's friend purred. I mean it, I really think she purred. Can humans purr? Seems I have a lot to learn about humans. Maybe they're not all mean.

"I know your precious Boo Boo and Trigger died recently," said this nice Sherry, "so I thought you might want to replace them with these three beauties."

"But I lost just two cats," the purring woman said, "and now you want me to take three?"

"Well we can't separate them from their mama can we?" Sherry said and I swear she was purring louder than the purr lady. What a saleswoman this Sherry is I thought to myself as I sat, hidden behind the closed door.

"Okay Sherry, you've got a deal. Who can resist kittens and this mama cat seems to have such a sweet nature," the purr lady said. "You know I'll give them a great forever home."

"I know that," Sherry smiled at Joan, and put my mama and my brother and sister back in the box that we had been found in, knowing that her friend would indeed take such good care of them.

I later learned that Sherry felt bad for not letting me go with my mama and brother and sister but she also knew that she was stretching it by asking her friend to take 3 cats. No way could she take four.

So off my mama and brother and sister went to live with this kind lady in a good home. I felt good about that. But I was secretly happy that I would be an "only cat" and have all the attention on just me… or so I thought.

I don't know why I was the one chosen to stay with Sherry and her family. Well, I always thought I was much prettier than my siblings but I kept that to myself. My mama knew what I thought though.

"You won't win any popularity contests if you brag about how handsome you are," my mama always said. She must have thought I was special too.

"What have we got here?" a big strange man said as he walked in the kitchen eyeballing me. I heard Sherry call him Jack and Scott called him dad so bingo! I figured that one out. I'm not your average cat. I always knew I was more than just my good looks. Got brains too!

So here I was; I was going to be living with Sherry, her husband Jack and Scott. I had no sooner started to plan how I was going to wrap these humans around my little paws, when another member of the house walked into the kitchen. I heard them call him Dale, and he was Scott's older brother. He came right over to me, picked me up and said "Well, what have we got here?"

"What you've got here, braniac," I thought to myself "is a kitten. Not only a kitten but by far the fairest kitten in the land. I'm special. Just ask Scott. Helloooo, haven't you ever seen a kitten before?"

Well those were my thoughts but I didn't dare say them out loud. I didn't want to get kicked out of this home too. I'd have to wait to see if they had a good sense of humor or not.

How did I go from being unwanted to being so lucky? I wondered. Oh well who cares, I'm here now and I'm stayin'.

As soon as Dale had put me down, Scott scooped me up and said "I'm going to call you Pumpkin because you're round and orange and I know you're going to grow to be a big fat cat." Nobody argued so Pumpkin I was.

Little did I know when Scott gently laid me down on the couch, that I would soon be greeted by other cats! Not only other cats but a big black dog. I mean she was the biggest dog I'd ever seen in my life, although I must admit I hadn't seen that many dogs in my short six weeks of life.

I decided I couldn't show any fear. I had to let the other cats and this big dog know who was boss. After all, I was special. I had been adopted. Whoo-hoo - I am the king of all felines! Everybody bow down to the Great Pumpkin.

Yes, I admit I liked the name that Scott gave me, although I thought Alexander the Great was a much nobler and fitting name for a cat of my beauty, grace and intelligence.

It wasn't until much later that I learned that Alexander the Great, King of Macedonia (a far away land near Greece) had become an alcoholic (someone who drinks too much alcohol and can't stop) and he died in a drinking binge (drinking a lot of alcohol at one time)! Oh the horror of it! Imagine - I could have been named after a man who was once one of the great rulers of all time, until he discovered alcohol, burned down cities, killed his best friend and lost his life at the young age of 33. Why, that's only about 5 years in cat years!

I didn't know that alcohol could cause people to do things like that. Of course there was a lot I didn't know then but I would slowly learn about alcohol and drugs and something called addiction.

Back to the big black dog and those other ordinary felines. As it turns out I didn't have to try to be brave because the dog was really just another pussycat. She weighed 115 pounds and could have smooshed me with one giant paw. But she was a gentle giant and she loved me right away. Well, what's not to love? I am totally adorable. Just ask me.

The other cats were tolerable. They didn't hiss at me or try to pick fights – most likely because they recognized that I was superior to them and much more handsome – but they were polite and shared their food with me.

Over the years we all got along very well and played rough and tumble with each other, quite often running and jumping and landing on the dog with a big thump! But the dog…oh by the way, I didn't tell you her name, it's Kazak, named after a dog in a Kurt Vonnegut story (a very popular author), Scott named her that, and she enjoyed watching us play.

Kazak, and my adopted sister and brother cats, Pippi, Taffy, Squeaky, Sugar, and Sly loved being inside cats. They were allowed in our big fenced in back yard to play but they really liked to stay inside.

Not me! I longed to be outside so I would try to follow Scott or Dale as they opened the door to go to school. Dale was wise to my tricks and always made sure that I stayed in the house.

Scott, on the other hand wanted to see how far I'd follow him if he let me outside. Well I showed him. I followed him all the way to The Square. It wasn't much of a walk but to me it was a big adventure.

Here I was, back to where I'd been found and adopted. It was very bittersweet. I missed my mama and my brother and sister. But I knew they had a good home and I had a loving home with humans who spoiled me rotten (as I so richly deserved) and they took care of all my health needs.

Okay, so I didn't like going to the vet – especially when they fixed me so I couldn't become a daddy, (they said something about there being too many homeless cats and dogs in the world) but they made sure I had all my shots so I wouldn't get sick.

My humans loved me but Scott loved me more than all the others. Maybe because he saw how special I am. Maybe because he admired my incredible beauty. Or maybe because he somehow knew that I understood him.

Scott and his brother Dale were extremely popular with all the kids who hung out in The Square. They could both play the guitar and they would bring their acoustic guitars to The Square and play them and sing. Everybody loved to hear them and to watch them. Those days were what I like to think of as The Good Times.

After school and at night after dinner, all the kids would walk to The Square and sit around on the park benches and listen to Scott and Dale play their guitars. The girls would dance to the music while some of the guys played air guitar. And everybody was texting somebody! Even texting the kids who were right there in The Square with them! I never could figure that one out but who really understands kids anyway? They're very special people, but not cat special of course!

I was happy because Scott would always let me follow him to The Square where I would be greeted by everyone as though I were the King of England, himself. Well, let's not be silly. The King of England would have to bow down to *me* if we met. I'm sure there is royalty in my background. I can just feel it. And I do carry myself in a most regal manner which the girls especially find amusing.

I would jump around from lap to lap being petted and stroked and cooed to as if I were a little baby. Kids being kids they always had food with them and there was usually something that I could eat, although I would sniff their offerings gingerly at first, waiting to hear them beg me to eat. Oh my, I had *them* eating out of *my* hand and they never knew it. Clever, aren't I?

What I remember most about The Good Times is that everybody had fun! There was a lot of laughing and good-natured kidding, eating and drinking sodas, telling jokes and of course complaining about teachers and homework. The dreaded homework.

"That Mr. Dunn is such a dork" somebody would say and everybody agreed with him. "All he cares about is how much homework he can give us."

"Well be glad you don't have Mr. Lewin" one of the girls moaned. "He's mean and hollers if we chew gum in his class."

I found this all to be very amusing. Just what the devil was homework anyway and what's a dork? And who would want to put sticky gum in their mouth and chew it? Yuck! The thought is enough to make me throw a hairball!

Nobody liked having a curfew either. They wanted to be out all night with their friends, just hangin' out and then when they went home they wanted to play games on their computers or email people or more texting. My goodness I've never seen anyone's fingers fly so fast as these texters!

How do they do that? I'll bet even if they had only paws like me, they could still text people with them and do it really fast. Kids are amazing.

The Good Times went on for many years. But slowly, over time, the kids grew older and became legally old enough to drive. There would be no more walking to The Square if they had their way. It didn't matter that it was only a couple of blocks to The Square. If they could beg their parents into letting them have the car, then they would drive there.

I didn't like riding in the car with Scott because I preferred to walk. Have to keep my perfect figure you know. But if I wanted to go to The Square for my daily pampering and Scott was driving I had to go with him.

But there was another reason I didn't want to ride in the car with Scott. I couldn't put my finger on it, I mean my paw on it, silly me, but I had a feeling that something was changing. I think somehow I knew that The Good Times were coming to an end.

SECTION TWO

The Monster Arrives

So…I've told you about my life from about six weeks of age up until now and it's been great, right? All fun and games.

Well it's easy to look back and see where things started to go so horribly wrong. But sometimes we're too close to situations to see what's happening. Some changes are bold and in your face but most changes are subtle. They occur slowly. Even if they're happening right under your nose, if you're not expecting them or looking for them, you may miss them.

I will always blame myself for not noticing how my wonderful Scott, my rescuer, started slipping away from his happy life and into a much darker place.

Scott had his own band, a really good one. He could play the guitar as well as any rock star. He had band practice at our house and the rec room was always filled with boys and girls. The girls would be screaming for Scott. He was almost as popular as I was. Well okay, I will admit that he probably was more popular than me…but not by much mind you!

Oh, he tried to imitate my look with his long wavy hair. But I had it all over him. Of course I would never let him know that. So I sat on the kitchen stool, watching his fingers dance so magically over the guitar strings, listening to the groupies – "Hey Scott, you're the bomb. You are jammin' man," and thinking how he had the world by the tail. Oh my, I made another funny. Humans don't have tails. I crack me up sometimes! But I knew Scott was going places. I still wasn't aware though that the places he was going would be jail and rehabs.

The Addiction Monster came creeping into our house. I sure wish he looked like a real monster, like a monster you'd see in the movies or on TV or video games. If he was, I could have clawed him and scratched his eyes out and saved my Scott, the one who saved me all those years ago.

No, the Monster wouldn't show himself to us, how ugly he really was inside. He was nice looking. Looked like any other kid in school. He smiled and talked to me and patted me on the head. He seemed nice. Even as smart as I am, I was fooled.

He had sneaked in, carried in by Luke, a member of Scott's band, Tantrum. Luke was the main singer for the band and I will admit he had really good stage presence. He would jump up on the furniture holding onto the microphone, screaming the words to whatever rock song they were playing. What he lacked in talent he made up for in sheer theatrics.

One day while Sherry and Jack weren't home – Dale was off with his own friends – I bounded into Scott's room where he and Luke were jamming out to some tune. I always liked to be where Scott was even though the loud music hurt my ears. It didn't matter. I was with Scott and would always be by his side. In some ways I was more like a dog than a cat but shhhhh, don't tell anyone that. I was loyal to Scott and he doted on me.

I don't know when it was that Scott started smoking cigarettes but I think it was when he was about 11 years old! I couldn't stand the smell and I wanted to tell Jack and Sherry but of course I can't speak the human language, even though I understand it very well, like most of my fellow felines and canines. You humans should remember that, the next time you're talking about taking us to the vet or giving us a pill. Why do you think we run and hide under the furniture? It's not for exercise. We know what you're up to. Silly humans, always trying to fool us four-legged critters.

So the smoking continued and Scott did a really good job of hiding the smell from Jack and Sherry. He was always brushing his teeth and washing his face and hands and changing his clothes. I imagine Jack and Sherry thought he was just really clean and careful about his hygiene and appearance.

Over time, and I'm not really sure when this started either, but the smell from the cigarettes started changing. It had a sweeter smell to it and it was just different. I don't know how to describe it other than I knew it wasn't tobacco that he was smoking now.

I could never understand why Scott smoked this stuff because when he first lit up the cigarette (which later I heard is called a "joint") he would choke and hack. The first time I witnessed this I truly thought he was going to die. I wondered how a human could have a hairball. I pranced up and down at his feet trying to save him. I wasn't sure how I was going to do this but I knew I had to try.

Within a minute though the hacking and coughing would stop and Scott would take another long drag (or "toke" as I would come to find out it's called) and he would smile and seem very mellow.

He'd really start talking to me then and would say really silly things and laugh. My, could that boy laugh…over nothing! Sometimes fits of laughter. I'd keep jumping around and he'd watch me and laugh even harder.

"Hey Pumpkin," Scott would say, "How are ya doin' buddy boy?"

"Is the weed making you laugh too?" Scott would ask me.

"Is that why you're having so much fun, dancing all around like a little circus animal? Well I'm putting you out of the room. This stuff isn't good for you," Scott said. Well if it wasn't good for me, how could it be good for him? I wondered.

I couldn't tell him why I was dancing, of course, it's that little language problem again, but I wanted to tell him that I wasn't dancing because I was happy. In fact I didn't even know why I was dancing. Something was making me dance and I didn't like it. I was losing control over my actions and that was not acceptable for a cat of my regal bearing. I was glad to leave the room.

Scott would then sneak down to the kitchen and raid the refrigerator and pantry. Sweet things seemed to be favored. He could eat half a gallon of ice cream in one sitting. Man, that boy is going to burst I'd worry.

He'd also do what I came to call the Mix and Match. He'd eat scoops of ice cream and then the next minute he'd be munching on a cold piece of chicken, and then on to something sweet again. Didn't matter what it was as long as it was tasty and there was plenty of it.

"Pumpkin, I've got major munchies" Scott would giggle. At first I wondered who this Major Munchies was. A new friend with an odd first name? Someone he was holding hostage? What was going on? I wondered where I could find this Major Munchies.

As I've said I'm not only outrageously handsome but also very, very intelligent. It didn't take too long to figure out that whenever Scott was smoking his weed, he would have the Major Munchies. Ah, got it now! That's what he called his really big appetite that overtook him after every joint.

I knew that if I were a human, I'd never smoke that stuff. First of all I was learning that smoke, any kind of smoke, tobacco smoke, pipe smoke or marijuana smoke was very, very bad for you. It could ruin your lungs and your heart and that major thought center – the Brain!

And scientists know that the human brain does not fully mature until humans are about 24 or 25 years old so they're ruining their brains before they've even really begun to mature. Would a cat do that? Of course not! We're much too smart.

In the beginning, I don't think Jack and Sherry ever realized what Scott was doing. He really hid his habit of smoking weed.

It was right around the same time he started smoking weed, that he began sneaking beer out of the refrigerator and bringing it up to his room, after the family had all gone to bed. He would sit on his bed, drinking beer, smoking weed and texting his friends. He kept quiet because he didn't want to wake anybody up.

I overheard Jack talking to Sherry one day, saying "I could swear I had a full six pack of beer in the refrigerator but one's missing. Funny, I don't remember drinking it. Hmmmmm…"

I couldn't tell them where that beer went but oh boy I wanted to. They never thought that Scott would be taking beer because he never had. And that, I began to see, is a problem.

Just because your kids have never given you any cause to not trust them, doesn't mean that you should always assume that they are innocent and trustworthy. Kids change. They grow up. They become teens. They make mistakes…sometimes really big ones.

Back to that day when I pranced into Scott's room. I saw a strange sight. I didn't know what was going on but it was sure strange. It was also Scott's 17th birthday. He would never know happy birthdays again.

Scott was hunched over his bedroom dresser and there was a long line of what looked like white powder and he was sniffing it up his nose. He'd sniff it, then make a horrible face and then he'd smile, pick up his guitar and rock on, full of wild energy. He and Luke did this for hours. I thought maybe it was some kind of new energy powder although I couldn't understand why he sniffed it instead of drinking it. I would soon find out.

The Monster was gaining a foothold in our once peaceful and loving home. I didn't like the Monster…but Scott seemed to love him…at first!

The Addiction Monster has many names. I've learned most of them but then it seems like every day there's another way to get "high" as I would overhear Scott say when talking to his friends.

That's another thing I couldn't understand…why would Scott call it getting "high" when after awhile it made him feel so "down?"

I heard names that I'd never heard of before like cocaine, heroin, crystal meth, acid, ecstasy, OxyContin, and so many more that my handsome little head was spinning like a top.

Then there's the "street names" for these drugs – Some of them are innocent sounding names like Ice, Chalk, Tina, Hug, Beans and a whole lot more. Way too many for me to remember or even want to. No matter what you call 'em, they all go by the same name – Death!

My Scotty Boy – my pet name for him – oh that's cute, I have a pet name for my human who isn't a pet, but I am. Now that's sort of like the twisted thinking that happens when you're on drugs. Uh oh, I hope I wasn't inhaling too much of that darn weed when I was in Scott's room. Not only is weed harmful to kids but it's also harmful to us pets.

I'm glad Scott never tried to get me "high" like I've heard that some people do to their pets. I'll always thank him for that…he never tried to harm me.

Anyway my Scotty Boy got thrown out of high school six weeks before graduation for stealing from other students to support his ever-growing drug habit. The drugs took his high school diploma from him.

Jack and Sherry never got to see him walk down that aisle with his cap and gown and diploma in hand. Was Scott stupid? Not academically. His last report card, the last one he received before being kicked out of school was straight A's. That's my Scotty Boy.

After kicking around from job to job and seeing that his drug habit was getting worse…he was now in full-blown addiction, Scott managed to join the Navy. He aced the test to get in and went to Great Lakes Naval Station. Believe it or not, he excelled there. We all thought this is it! Scott has seen how bad drugs are and he's turning his life around.

He was assigned to the Navy Color Guard and when he graduated from boot camp Jack and Sherry flew out there to see him. They were so proud.

They took a lot of pictures which I saw when they returned home. I'd never seen him look so handsome. Yes, he actually might have been even more handsome than me, all dressed up in his Navy uniform. Imagine if they had uniforms for cats! I would be dazzling.

While in the Navy Scott was trained as a Hospital Corpsman and he loved it. He had carried his dad's Anatomy and Physiology book around with him ever since he was big enough to hold it. It weighed a lot.

Scott got transferred to Bethesda Naval Hospital where he got to take care of patients. He told me he really loved to do that. He wanted to be a doctor one day. He loved helping people. Scott was kind. The Addiction Monster is cruel.

Well you know how luck goes…it's either good or bad and Scott's bad luck was to have a roommate who turned out to be a drug dealer. What a combination – a drug dealer and an addicted person sharing a room. It wasn't long before Scott was doing drugs again and stealing so he could buy more drugs.

It was a sad day at our house when the call came that Scott had to go through something called a Courts Martial. I'm not really sure what it is because I don't think cats go through these things, but I know it was bad. I remember Sherry crying so hard on the phone and there was nothing I could do but rub up against her legs and purr, hoping she understood that I was trying to console her.

I missed my Scotty Boy so bad. He spent six months in the Navy prison in Charleston, South Carolina. When he came home I was so happy to see him that I danced; only this was really a happy dance, not a drug dance. My rescuer was home and we'd be together again. That's all I cared about.

Things were good…for awhile. Scott and his beautiful girlfriend studied to be EMTs – Emergency Medical Technicians. Scott graduated first in his class. We were all so proud of him.

Then he went to community college and graduated as a Paramedic. We didn't think we could be any happier. Our Scotty Boy loved being a Paramedic and saving lives.

Then in May, about two years later, our proudest moment in Scott's career came, when Jack and Sherry and Dale and Dale's and Scott's grandfather watched as Scott received his nursing pin. He was now a Registered Nurse.

Being a male nurse I called him a Murse which I thought was pretty darn funny…and clever. But that shouldn't surprise you because I told you how smart I am. I wasn't kidding was I?

The years had passed since that first day when Scott was given cocaine for his 17th birthday present by his band mate, Luke. Scott was in and out of jail for stealing to buy drugs.

Jack and Sherry put him in rehab when he was 17. They did it as soon as they found out about his problem. That was the first of 5 rehabs that he would be in throughout his life. They tried so hard to save him. But the Monster was trying harder to keep him on drugs. The Monster won!

Our once happy home where everybody laughed and had fun, had now become a nightmare. Everything in our home now revolved around drugs and Scott…how to stop Scott from using them, how to stop Scott from stealing, how to stop him from hanging around other people who used drugs.

Sometimes Scott would leave the house and be gone for 2 days and not let us know where he was. He wouldn't even tell me! I hated when he did that because it made Sherry and Jack so sad. And it would make them fight with each other. I may be a cat but I knew the reason they were fighting was because they were so frustrated and scared to death that something bad would happen to Scott.

Most of the time though I saw Jack hugging Sherry trying to comfort her, telling her that everything would be okay and she would stop crying. Then the phone would ring and we would all jump!

Was it Scott calling to let us know that he was okay? Was it the police calling to tell us he'd been in an accident? Was it the hospital calling to say he was in the Emergency Room?

Sherry couldn't run to the phone quickly enough. The color would drain from her face as she picked up the phone and I could see her hands shaking. Jack would be right beside her with his ear to the phone waiting to find out if the call was from or about our beloved Scotty Boy.

I could tell right away if the call was good news or bad news by the look on Sherry's face. It was always such a big relief when they would hear Scott's voice on the phone. It's strange but Sherry would sometimes cry even harder after she hung up the phone.

I understood that this was a human response to the emotion of relief. They were so happy to know that our boy was alive but so sad that the Addiction Monster had once again kidnapped him and made him do things that he never did before – before the Monster invaded his mind and body.

We all loved Scott, just as much as we love his brother Dale. We understood that Scott had a disease. The disease is called addiction and it's a brain disease. You can avoid getting this brain disease yourself by never, ever trying drugs. Never ever! Once you choose to do drugs, it may be the last choice you will ever make. The drugs will now make all the decisions.

My Scotty Boy was a good kid. He was so kind and generous. He shared whatever he had with Dale and all his friends. He was kind to me and to everybody.

It is the drugs that are bad, not the person using them. But the drugs make good people do bad things like stealing. This is why people should never do drugs! Why can't people be like cats? Or even dogs? I don't understand why people want to do drugs knowing the bad things that drugs make them do.

They say the drugs make them feel good but from what I've seen, that good feeling is only for a short time and then they get sad and depressed.

Then they need more drugs again to make them feel good. They are out of control. Who wants that?

I would watch Scott pacing the floor, full of nervous energy. Sometimes he would sit on the floor and pick at things that weren't there. That would really scare me. I would walk over to where he was picking and stare at the floor but I couldn't see anything. But Scott would keep picking and picking. I thought my boy was losing his mind…and in a way I guess he was.

Scott told me later when the drugs were cleared from his head that picking at things is a side effect of doing certain drugs. I think even if I did have nine lives I would never fully understand humans. And you know what? I would never want to be one! Cats rule!

My Scotty Boy had gone from using cocaine, to crack cocaine and then to heroin, that awful, horrible heroin. I listen to the TV and radio a lot and I learned that heroin comes from the poppy flower. I don't understand how such a beautiful flower can produce something that can cause such a horrible death and such sadness.

I know there are some kids who don't believe that you can become addicted the first time you try a drug. They think their parents or the schools are lying to them. Well if you won't listen to your parents or to your teachers or guidance counselors, then please listen to me – the cat! ***You can definitely become addicted to drugs the first time you try them. Believe it!***

Why would any human want to take that chance? Too bad they can't all be cats. Why, I don't even sniff catnip now because I'm afraid I might become addicted. Why take that chance? Hey! Don't laugh at the cat. I think I hear you giggling but it's nothing to laugh about. Drugs will ruin your life. No joke.

I told you in the beginning that I am very smart. I learned the hard way, by watching my beloved Scotty Boy fall deeper and deeper into addiction, that this happened because he tried cocaine that one time. Yes, that was all it took! From that day on he couldn't get enough of that death drug or the heroin that followed.

He craved drugs and the drugs completely took over his life. If he could talk to you, he would tell you not to make the same mistake that he made. He would beg you not to do drugs. He put up a good fight. I saw him try to beat it. We talked about drugs a lot. Well actually Scott did all the talking of course, me being a cat and all that. I just listened. We would sit on his bed and he'd be stroking my head and looking very sad.

He used to say to me "Pumpkin, I'm going to beat this. I'll never do drugs again. Look at what they've done to my life. I have no life now. It's all about the drugs. From the time I get up until I go to sleep that's all I can think of...how to get money to buy more drugs. I just want to have my life back and to be a kid again and have fun."

I cried for Scott in my own cat way. Maybe he couldn't see the tears but I felt them. I knew I was going to lose my best friend, the boy who had rescued me from possible death. Now it was my turn to try to rescue him and the sad part is that I couldn't. Nobody could. Not Jack and Sherry, not even himself.

The Scott we all knew and loved really had started to die on his 17th birthday. It took him 14 long years of struggle, trying to beat that terrible Addiction Monster but the Monster was much stronger. It fought back with all its might.

I told you in the beginning of the book that the Monster doesn't have big scary fangs, red eyes or horns. He has something much worse, much scarier. He has power over you, absolute and total power. He controls your life and you can't do anything about it.

He takes everything from you and he doesn't care how much he hurts you or your family…or me, the cat.

In the wee early hours of the morning on Monday, December 2nd, our household was awakened by the phone ringing. It was the police calling us from their cell phone. They were standing outside our front door and wanted Sherry and Jack to open the door.

I trembled, not knowing why the police were at our house at 1:15 in the morning. We had all been sound asleep, snug in our bed. I was stretched out between Sherry and Jack, warm and comfy, and was having a really good dream. I was dreaming that my Scotty Boy had beaten the Addiction Monster and we were all so happy. We had our boy back again. No more living in fear every day that he would die from drugs. What a great dream! But that's all it was, a dream.

Sherry ran to the door and opened it, followed quickly by Jack. I stayed in bed because I was too scared to see what was going on. I didn't want to know why the police were at our house. I didn't know what was going on but I knew it was not good. And I knew it involved Scott.

The next thing I heard was a heartbreaking scream and Sherry yelling No!, No!, No!, over and over again. And then Jack yelling No!, No!, too. I told you I'm a smart cat so I knew right away that our worst nightmare had come true.

I just wanted to go back to sleep, back to my wonderful dream and stay in bed forever. But my family needed me now. They needed something warm and furry and fluffy to pick up and stroke, to be comforted by. So I purred my loudest purr and rubbed against them and hoped we could get through this...a life now without our Scotty Boy.

On December 1, 2002 I lost my best friend. Jack and Sherry lost their youngest son. Dale lost his only brother. None of us will ever see that beautiful smile again or those big brown eyes. We'll never hear him play his guitar again. We'll never be playfully teased by him again. We'll never go to The Square together again. All because of drugs!

Christmas is an especially rough time in our house. Scott died just 3 weeks before Christmas. Christmas Eve was always his favorite night of the year and we'd all sit around the tree, listening to the Christmas Carols, eagerly anticipating what gifts were in those beautifully wrapped boxes.

There were even Christmas stockings with all of

our names on them. Of course I had the best stocking, being the favorite and all.

They all loved to watch me and my adopted brothers and sisters running full steam ahead into the tree and climbing up inside it. They didn't get angry with us. They laughed. We were so adorable. Yes, they were The Good Times.

You may think Scott was old because he was 31 when he died, but when you grow up you'll see how young that really is. My Scotty Boy had his whole life ahead of him.

He accomplished a lot of things even though he was addicted but the one thing that he wanted to accomplish most of all, he couldn't. He could not beat the Addiction Monster.

I haven't been back to The Square in all these years since the drugs took my Scotty Boy away from me. The place where I had known so much happiness now just makes me sad to think about.

The Square has changed too, I've been told. Where kids used to play music and sing and dance, they now hang out on the park benches doing drugs and drinking, vomiting on themselves when they've overdone it and passing out…and some dying. For some strange reason they think they're really cool. I don't know what's so cool about dying. A lot of people are working very hard on making The Square a really nice place again, where families (and handsome cats) are not afraid to go after dark.

Kazak, our big black lab goes for walks to The Square with Sherry and Jack. She came home from her walk one day and was very sad. She told me (yes we animals can communicate with each other in a way that humans don't understand) some very sad news.

Kazak was listening to Sherry and Jack talk to some of the kids in The Square, begging them not to do drugs. They were saying that they didn't want any other kids to die and they didn't want any other parents to have their hearts broken.

Sadly, they found out that many of the kids had also died from an overdose of drugs. Even though they had all been to the D.A.R.E. classes at school and had heard about how drugs take control of your life, these kids still didn't believe it. Some of the kids were from Fairview and some were from the next town called Morgan Village and some were from the bigger town called Camden. But they all had one thing in common – deadly drugs!

They found out that Mike, who had played football on the 8th grade team, got involved with drugs. He was going to go to college and he wanted to be a Sports Medicine doctor. He died of a mixture of OxyContin pills and cocaine.

Maria was beautiful, with long legs and beautiful red hair and dazzling green eyes that looked like emeralds. She was going to be an actress and everybody knew she would be famous. Now she was dead from heroin.

De'Shante' was a really outgoing kid who everybody loved. He even had a part-time job after school, working at the local library. He was super smart and was going to go to college, get his law degree and run for public office one day, perhaps be a senator or congressman. He wanted to reach out and help people.

De'Shante' had an older brother who made Crystal Meth in the family's basement. He talked De'Shante' into taking some. De'Shante' knew he shouldn't do it but he was a kid. He wanted to try it because his big brother said how good it made you feel. He always did whatever his big brother told him to do. He thought he would try it once and that would be it. But he liked it and kept doing it. It wasn't too long before the family found him in the basement lying perfectly still on the floor. There would never be a Senator or Congressman named De'Shante'. The Crystal Meth saw to that!

Eddie wanted to be a teacher. He was one of the smartest boys who hung out in The Square. Eddie had no self-esteem. He thought that the other kids didn't like him and if he did drugs they would think he was cool. Eddie died from a mixture of Methadone and Xanax pills.

Antoine (or Tony as everybody called him) was

tall, way taller than anybody else in his class and he was a really good basketball player. He was fast and could jump high and always scored the most baskets. Everybody cheered for Tony when he walked out on the basketball court. Tony just knew he was going to be a Center for some big team, maybe the Boston Celtics or the Miami Heat.

Tony said he'd make everybody forget about Michael Jordan or Shaquille O'Neal. He was going to be better than them. He thought if he took steroids it would help him be an even better athlete. He didn't tell anybody that his uncle was giving him the steroids. He wanted them all to think that he was just naturally good and strong. Everybody found out about his steroid use though after he was found dead in the school gym.

Josh was handsome and brilliant. He was a musician and also wanted to be an engineer. His dad was an engineer so he was going to be just like his dad. One day he found some Valium pills in the medicine cabinet and for reasons known only to him, he took several Valiums and stole liquor from the kitchen cabinet. His family found him on the kitchen floor. He had died from the mixture of pills and alcohol.

Brent developed a drinking problem. He would get drunk before going to school! One day he bought some pills – some OxyContin – from a so-called friend of his and he swallowed a few along with his morning alcohol. He never even made it to the school bus. His mom found him in his bedroom. She thought he had overslept. She tried to wake him up. He would never wake up again, dead from alcohol and pills.

Then there was Brittany, a cheerleader at the local school, Yorkship school, a couple of blocks from The Square. She was really popular and wanted to work in the government as a diplomat. She had the perfect combination of brains and good looks. She also discovered drugs – LSD, or acid as the kids call it. She began having hallucinations and one day jumped out of her third story window to get away from the monsters that were chasing her in her head. She was in a coma for 9 days before her parents had to have her life support taken away. The whole family sat around her bedside and held her hands and watched as she quietly died.

Joey was a dirt bike racer who wanted to be a pilot in the Air Force when he grew up. He had an accident with the bike and got hurt real bad. The hospital gave him pain pills. He liked the pain pills and started taking more and more of them and when he ran out of the pills, he bought more from drug dealers on the street. One day he took too many. He never woke up.

Kaitlyn studied very hard in school and wanted to be a lawyer just like her mother, father and uncle. She sure had the brains to go to law school. But one night she went to a "pharm" party. My little cat ears thought they were talking about a "farm" party. I wondered what could be so bad about a farm party.

I found out that "pharm" parties are where kids steal pills from their parents' medicine cabinet and they all get together and put all the pills in a bowl and mix them up. Then the kids take a handful of pills and swallow them, usually swallowing them with alcohol. What? How can that be? I asked myself. Who would do such a stupid thing? They don't even know what these pills are! Some are uppers and some are downers. They can kill you! Kaitlyn found that out...the hard way. The Emergency Room doctors could not save her.

If only I could speak their language, I would tell them how they are wasting the only life they'll ever have. You don't get nine lives, you don't get two lives, you get just one.

You all know how smart I am. I mean I keep telling you often enough. But as smart as this handsome little cat is, I've gotta tell you, I can't figure out why some kids do drugs. Why do they want to throw their only life away? Don't they know they can become addicted? They can become a slave to the Addiction Monster? It makes me so crazy that I run over to my scratching post and scratch and scratch and scratch, trying to vent all my frustrations. My people think I'm really into exercise. But I'm not. I just don't know what else to do.

I heard Sherry telling Scott many times, "Enjoy life Scott. This is not a dress rehearsal. You can't have a good life when you do drugs." She wanted him to be happy and live a long life. I know Scott wanted that too but the drugs stole his future. The drugs stole everything from everybody in my family and they stole my happiness too.

As for me, I go on and I enjoy my life as much as I can, being pampered by everybody in the family. They pet me and cuddle me and I sometimes catch them looking at me with a sad look on their face. They can tell that I miss Scott too.

I hear Sherry and even Jack crying sometimes. They try to hide their sadness from me but things are different now. I hate those drugs! Look what they did to our happy family. Look what they did to our Scotty Boy.

Dale gives me extra attention and lets me sleep in his room now. He has a big picture of Scott on his dresser so I can look at that each night before I go to sleep. I love Dale and Sherry and Jack but I really loved my Scotty Boy.

Sometimes when I'm sitting on the bed with Dale, he talks to me. He tells me how much he misses Scott and how sad he is that he doesn't have a brother anymore. He tells me how much he loved him and how he tried to stop him from doing drugs, but even he couldn't help him. I understand how he feels. None of us could help our Scotty Boy.

So I gently stand on his lap and look up at him with my beautiful big green eyes and then I rub my head against his face. He strokes my head and says "You're a great cat, Pumpkin. Thanks for listening. I wish you knew how I'm feeling but somehow I think you do."

I just purr louder and make little squeaky sounds, happy that Dale confides in me and happy that he knows I understand. We will get through this together somehow. We may have lost our Scotty Boy but we haven't lost our love for him. We will remember him every day and will always be sad that we lost him. And we will beg every kid we meet not to do drugs because drugs ruin lives.

I made a silent promise to Scott on the night that he died. Well okay I know what you're saying – of course I made a silent promise. I'm a cat! I can't speak! But you know what I mean.

I promised Scott that as long as I lived I would somehow tell others all about the Addiction Monster and how big and mean and scary this real monster is. Now that you know what really happens when you do drugs, please tell others. Tell them about my beloved Scotty Boy.

If your friends try to get you to do drugs please tell them No! You can have a good life and a great future...or you can have drugs. You can't have both. Know how to say No!

So even though you've never met me in person I'm going to ask a really big favor of you. Please promise me that you will never throw your life and your future away on drugs and alcohol. Hey, and no gambling. That can become a big addiction too!

Make that promise to yourself, to your family, to your friends and relatives, to Scott and if you wouldn't mind, make that promise to me – The Square Cat, Pumpkin the Great, the most handsome animal who ever lived, the smartest and most lovable cat in the whole world; and the cat who loves you just as you are.

I'm ending my little cat tale (clever, huh? tale/tail) with these very wise words that a friend of Sherry's said. I always hear Sherry saying to any kid who will listen – Be smart, don't start. But her friend wanted you to remember these words too because they are so important.

Please Read and Remember this —

Taking drugs is EASY—but stopping drugs—is HARD. Once the Addiction Monster gets you, it's too late.

Be smart – Don't start

Well here I am—The real Square Cat—
Pumpkin The Great. As you can see I'm not
square. I'm beautiful and fluffy with big green eyes.
Thank you for reading my story about my
Scotty Boy. And be sure to tell all your friends—
Be Smart – Don't Start!

Picture of Scott in his Navy uniform and mom wearing his "dixie cup." Mom was so proud of our Scotty Boy.

Sheryl Letzgus McGinnis is the author of *I Am Your Disease (The Many Faces of Addiction)*, her first book, written after the tragic death of her youngest son, Scott Graeme McGinnis, RN from a drug overdose.

Sheryl has been interviewed on radio stations, satellite radio, and TV. She has spoken at her local library on drug addiction and has several speaking engagements coming up in the fall of 2008. She is an Expert Platinum Author on the internet site www. Ezine.com and writes many articles on addiction and has also been a featured Op-Ed writer for a Mother's Day piece in the *Florida Times Union*. Other articles by her have appeared in *Florida Today*.

Slaying the Addiction Monster is her second book. It has stories in it from moms and dads who have lost their precious child to the Addiction Monster. The book also has advice from moms and dads who want other parents to know what signs to look for if they think their child might be using drugs. There is information on addiction research and just about anything you'd want to know about drugs today.

Simultaneously while writing *Slaying the Addiction Monster*, she also wrote this book, *The Addiction Monster and the Square Cat*, a fictionalized version of her son Scott's descent into the world of drugs, his long struggle to overcome the addiction and his ultimate death.

Sheryl is a retired medical transcriptionist and a former radio DJ and voice-over artist who now lends her voice to speaking out about drugs. She is married to retired science teacher, Jack McGinnis. Their son Dale, lives nearby and is a full time grad student. The McGinnises are owned by 1 beautiful lab, (their son Scott's dog,) and 4 spoiled cats. They live in Palm Bay, Florida. Sheryl is always available to speak about addiction. She is on the Parent Advisory Board of the Partnership For a Drug-Free America.

3260084

Made in the USA